Get the Gum

by Susan Hartley • illustrated by Anita DuFalla

"Can you get the bag of gum for me, Tam?" said Gus.

"No, Gus, I cannot get the gum for you," said Tam. "I am on the rug."

"Can you get the gum for me, Ben?" said Gus.

"No, I cannot get the gum for you, Gus," said Ben. "I am at the pen with Mem."

"No gum for me," said Gus.

The pup can see the gum.
The pup can get the gum.

"See the pup!" said Gus.
"The pup has the bag of gum. No, pup.
You cannot have the gum."